To the Phil
W9-AAW-197

TESSA DAHL

SCHOOL can wait

ILLUSTRATED BY KORKY PAUL

VIKING

Also by Tessa Dahl

Gwenda And The Animals
illustrated by Korky Paul
The Same but Different
illustrated by Arthur Robins

VIKING
Published by the Penguin Group
Viking Penguin, a division of Penguin Books USA Inc.,
375 Hudson Street, New York, New York 10014, U.S.A.
Penguin Books Ltd, 27 Wrights Lane, London W8 5TZ, England
Penguin Books Australia Ltd, Ringwood, Victoria, Australia
Penguin Books Canada Ltd, 10 Alcorn Avenue, Toronto, Ontario, Canada M4V 3B2
Penguin Books (N.Z.) Ltd, 182–190 Wairau Road, Auckland 10, New Zealand
Penguin Books Ltd, Registered Offices: Harmondsworth, Middlesex, England
First published in Great Britain by Hamish Hamilton, 1990
First published in the United States of America, 1991

1 3 5 7 9 10 8 6 4 2

ISBN 0-670-84170-6
Printed in the U.S.A.

To my dearest teacher
Gurumayi Chidvilasananda
and all her pupils everywhere

Chapter One

Jack is eight. He is very average for his age. He is "average size". He is "average brains" and he is "average at sports".

He is also bored of being "average".

This is Jack's mum. She is very average. She also worries a great deal – about everything.

This is Jack's dad. He is very average – he also does everything Jack's mum says.

Jack feels as if he is stuck in sticky glue. Because, as much as he loves his mum and his dad, he longs for adventure.

He wishes he could flick a switch and turn his parents on.

5

One Sunday – like every Sunday – Jack's dad took him up to the woods to play Indians. The mud squelched under Jack's boots. It was a crackly morning.

"How do you know where I'm hiding, Dad?" asked Jack.

"Because it's so cold I can hear you."

"What do you mean?" Jack was fed up. He was bored of being found.

"When it's shivery freezing the woods give you away. If I stand quietly and listen I can hear the bushes crackle or the twigs snap. I can hear the crispy leaves under your feet. Stand still, Jack, and listen."

Jack stood still. He held his breath. A robin was rummaging around on the ground. It sounded as if it was searching through a pile of horrible, hard school lavatory paper, not lovely brown leaves.

But what was *that* noise?

Jack looked at his dad. Dad looked at Jack. It was a crunchy, snappy sound coming from the hawthorn bush.

"Come on, Jack, let's investigate. It could be a fox."

They crept over to the bush. Dad lifted Jack up and Jack peered through the twigs.

There in front of him, right there, staring at Jack, was a reindeer. His antlers were sticking out of the top of the bush. They looked like branches.

"It's a reindeer, Dad," whispered Jack.

Jack's dad poked his face into the bush. "You're right, it *is* a reindeer."

"Stop staring and help me," the reindeer said. "I'm stuck in this tangly mess and I can't get out."

Jack and his dad pushed the branches away. The twigs and leaves snapped and rustled.

"At last," sighed the reindeer, as it stepped on to the path. They all stood there – Jack, Dad and the reindeer.

"How do you do? Blitzen's the name."

"I'm Jack and this is my dad."

"You cannot believe how pleased I am to see you. I've been lost in this wood for days. I'd quite given up."

"How did you get here?" asked Dad.

"Well, it was my fault. On Christmas Eve, Father Christmas – I work for him, you see – stopped at the cottage down the hill there. We'd been terribly busy delivering presents to all the boys and girls and I was a bit fed up and hungry. Father Christmas had gone down the

chimney and while we were waiting I noticed a delicious holly bush. I asked Prancer to undo my reins and told him I'd be back in a minute. Behind the first holly bush was an even bigger one, so I trotted over and tucked in. I was busy munching away and I didn't notice Father Christmas come back when suddenly above my head I heard the sleigh and bells. 'Wait for me,' I shouted. But they were off – Father Christmas hadn't noticed."

"That's awful," said Jack.

Blitzen stooped his head. "It is awful. It's quite ghastly. I've been here for days, wandering around and I'm homesick."

Dad put his arm around Blitzen's neck and stroked his nose. "Don't worry, we'll get you home."

Back at the house, Mum made Blitzen some tea and gave him the comfiest chair by the fire. Dad was on the phone, booking their plane tickets. Jack was packing his bag.

"You won't need to pack much," shouted Mum. "We'll be back for school on Monday."

I don't think so, thought Jack. *I don't think so.*

Chapter Two

Jack sat on the aeroplane next to Blitzen. He had never been on a plane before, because Mum was frightened of flying. Now she didn't seem scared at all. The man behind Blitzen was complaining loudly that he couldn't see the film because Blitzen's antlers were in the way.

Jack's mum turned around and said kindly but firmly, "I'm afraid there's no point making a fuss because there's nothing we can do about it."

Blitzen tried to scrunch down in his seat but it really didn't work. By the time they reached the North Pole he was rather grumpy.

"I can't think why all you humans take aeroplanes," he sniffed as he led Jack, Mum and Dad to Father Christmas's house. "Our sleigh is much smoother."

"They don't serve Coca-Cola on the sleigh," Jack said, "and you wouldn't have a film, either."

It was far colder than they had been expecting and far spookier. The ground was covered in crunchy snow. It was a lonely, icy, white land, with no houses or trees. Jack's mum was wearing the wrong shoes.

"Really, Blitzen," she scolded. "You could have told me to wear my boots. After all, to be forewarned is to be forearmed."

"Get on my back, all of you. It's not far now, and once we get there Mother Christmas will dry your stockings."

They all clambered on to Blitzen's back. They hung on to each other and joggled about, with the wind whistling between their shivery bodies.

They trotted up a hill and when they reached the top Blitzen stopped. It was a fantastic sight. Tucked into the side of a huge snowy mountain sat a tiny cottage. There was smoke coming out of the chimney and flickers of yellow light inside the window.

Blitzen galloped down the steep slope – Jack, Mum and Dad had to cling on tightly as he went so fast. Blitzen stopped at the gate and Dad whispered in Jack's ear, "We are about to meet Father Christmas. No one will ever believe us."

Jack couldn't speak. His brain had gone fuzzy with excitement. He felt he was in the middle of a sandwich, stuck on top of Blitzen, between Mum and Dad. An adventure sandwich, he thought, as Blitzen's antlers banged against the door, and the latch went up.

And there *he* was. With no shoes on, and a pipe tucked in his mouth. He had a red cardigan and black trousers. But Jack knew it was him all right. Father Christmas peered out into the darkness and suddenly realized it was his reindeer, come home.

"Oh, Blitzen – I thought we'd lost you forever. This is good news indeed. Mother Christmas, look who's here."

"Father Christmas, may I introduce you to my new friends," said Blitzen – rather politely, Jack noticed.

"Of course, of course, do come in, please do."

It was dark in the kitchen. Candles were burning and there were wonderful smells coming from the stove.

Mother Christmas busied around, drying Mum's stockings and making cocoa, while Father Christmas sat at the end of the table and listened to Blitzen's story.

"Hm, that'll teach you to be greedy," he laughed. "The times I've caught him eating the holly wreaths on people's doors."

"Now, as for you lot, you must spend the night. We insist, don't we, Mother?"

"It's very kind," said Jack's mum. "But we should get going. Jack has school on Monday."

Mother Christmas was whispering something to her husband. Then she started pointing to the shelves. Jack could tell she was trying to do it without any of them noticing.

"What *are* you doing, my dear?" asked Father Christmas.

"You know, dearest," she hissed loudly. "Our little problem."

"Oh yes, our little problem," muttered Father Christmas.

"Well, I thought they could help us," explained Mother Christmas.

"Good thinking, very good thinking. Yes, yes. We've got a bit of a favour to ask. A nut we need to crack."

Jack could not believe his ears. Father Christmas was asking *them* a favour.

"When I got back here on Christmas Day," explained Father Christmas, "I was exhausted. I had been out way past my usual going-home time because of Blitzen – the sleigh took much longer as we were one reindeer short. I'd been into the house and had some tea, and then I wandered back to the stables to check on the other reindeer. As I walked in I was hit by the most disgusting smell. It was foul. Far worse than I'd ever smelt before. Horrible. I started to check the sleigh and I noticed that the smell was coming from under the seat. Holding my nose, I peered down, and there, curled up and terrified, was a little skunk."

"A *what*?" asked Jack's dad.

"A skunk. They're American animals. They live in the woods. Rather sweet and pretty with bushy tails and a long white stripe down their black backs. But when they're frightened they let off the most revolting ponk. I persuaded the skunk to come out. Harry, he said his name was."

"But how did he get in your sleigh?" Jack was fascinated.

"It seems that he saw us land in the Smokey Mountains – that's in America, way down south – and thought it would be fun to stow away. Of course he didn't stop to think, and by the time I got home he was petrified."

"Poor little thing," whispered Mum.

"The problem is that he's homesick. The North Pole is no place for a skunk. He tries to be good, but he can't help being naughty. He's driving Mother Christmas up the wall. He rummages in the rubbish and when she gets cross he lifts his tail and out comes the most terrible ponk. So, what we're hoping is that you'll get him back to America for us."

"Where is he now?" asked Jack's dad.

"I'm here," said a squeaky voice from somewhere near the ceiling. Jack looked up, searching the dark rafters. He didn't know what a skunk looked like, but he wanted to see it. He liked the sound of this creature who could scare people off by making a revolting stink. He thought how useful it would be at school.

"I'm here, look up on the shelves," said the little voice.

"Oh, what a poppet." Jack's mum had caught sight of Harry and she walked over to the shelves and lifted him down into her arms.

"That's a matter of opinion," sniffed Mother Christmas. They sat at the table, Harry cradled on Mum's chest like a baby. They worked out a plan.

"I'll take you to the airport on the sledge," said Father Christmas, "and Mother can pop in and see her friend at Pole Air – I'm sure they'll take good care of you all, won't they, Mother?"

"Oh yes, you can be sure of that," replied Mother Christmas, with a smile. "After all, everyone wants to keep on the right side of the Christmases."

Jack imagined his classroom, all his friends sitting at their desks, while his sat there empty.

Mum's words jolted him back as he heard her say with a sigh, "Oh well, nothing ventured, nothing gained." It seemed funny, he thought, that all Mum's little sayings meant something different now that they were on an adventure.

Chapter Three

Harry behaved beautifully on the plane. Jack's mum wore him around her neck and no one even noticed – he looked just like a fur collar. She had made him promise not to make a ponk and he kept his word. Harry was so happy to be going home.

As they flew over the edge of the Smokey Mountains they gasped. It was beautiful – far more beautiful than they could have believed possible.

"This is America, Jack," whispered Dad. "This is the most exciting country."

"I really do hope we can get you home in time for school tomorrow, Jack," said Jack's mum with a sigh, as they got off the plane. "Come along, Harry, we're not here on holiday, you know."

Jack, Jack's mum, Jack's dad and Harry all piled into a taxi and trundled down to the end of a dusty road on the edge of the Smokey Mountains.

"Follow me," squeaked Harry, as he scampered off. The pine needles under their feet made a very different noise from crunchy English leaves. Jack felt as if he was walking on a thick, springy, softer-than-sponge carpet. The woods smelt like hundreds and hundreds of sweet Christmas trees. Harry kept running ahead, doing a sort of skipping dance, and then turning around to check on his new friends. "Please hurry, I want to see my family so badly," Harry called back to them. "We're nearly there, just two more corners and three more giant oak trees."

"That's what they are, Jack," Dad marvelled. "Look up. Stand at the bottom of the trunk and put your arms around it – then gaze up. Pretty amazing, eh?"

Jack and his dad stood hugging the giant oak, chins in the air. The branches looked like the arms of an enormous giant with the sky behind them.

"What on earth are you two up to?" asked Mum.

"Try it, Mum," said Jack.

Mum looked tempted. "No, I don't think I will – I don't want to mess up my dress. Come on now, we really must get a move on."

But then she stopped – and started to smile.
"All right, why not?" she said – almost to herself.
And there they stood, all three of them, with their arms wrapped around the tree. For a moment it was like the end of a dance, just as the music stops. And then, as if the band had finished and the dance was over, they all let go of their enormous partner.

Running, they caught up with Harry, who had just stopped under a very large oak tree.

"This is my house," he squealed. "Ma, Pa, Lavinia, I'm home," he shouted down a hole.

Jack, Mum, Dad and Harry all stood still. There was a scuffling sound, a scratching noise and then a nose poked up, followed up by two little bright eyes.

"Harry – oh my dearest baby, we thought you were gone for ever."

Harry's mum hugged him tightly, licking and licking his face. While Jack watched, he thought how odd it would be if *his* mum licked *his* face.

Harry's pa came out of the hole next. "Where've you been, son?" he asked.

Harry started to tell his incredible story. While he was telling it, his sister Lavinia joined them – wide-eyed with admiration.

At the end of the tale Harry's pa turned to Jack's family and announced, "We're mighty grateful to you folks. This skunk of ours has been naughty but that's in the past. We're just blessed to have him home. Now, Ma, what can we do to thank these goodly people?"

"Well, Pa, they wouldn't be comfortable here, but I've an idea they'd like it up at the White House."

Jack thought he hadn't heard properly. "The White House?" he spluttered.

"Yup," she answered with a grin. "Pa here has an uncle who is some kind of mascot up in Washington. The President's very fond of animals, and one of his dogs tried to kill Uncle George when they were out this way once so the President and his wife took George home to be cared for. Tell you what, we'll send one of the pigeons off to spread the word – an advance party, so to speak – and you'll be treated like royalty."

Jack felt quivery. First Father and Mother Christmas, and now the President of America, the White House, Washington. It was tingling his toes!

"I really think we should get Jack back to school," said Mum.

"I just won't hear of it" – insisted Harry's ma.

"We would be mortified unless you allowed us to show you our thanks," added Harry's pa.

Chapter Four

"The President will see you now," said a tall man with dark glasses in a dark suit.

Jack, Mum and Dad were led into a large oval office. Behind the huge desk sat the President and beside the President sat a skunk.

"How do you do," said the President.

"How do you do?" said the skunk.

"How do you do?" said Jack, Mum and Dad all at once.

"Our skunk George here has told me about your adventures. Your kindness is an example to all Americans. I know that old codger Father Christmas, and you can be sure he'd have had poor little Harry working alongside his elves, if it weren't for Harry's stink. You can bet your bottom dollar Harry would not have been brought home until next Christmas. By then his paws would have been raw with all that sewing and wrapping. Oh yes, he's quite a trickster, old Father Christmas."

"Harry was clever, though," interrupted George. He ponked his way out."

"Yes, sirree," laughed the President. "I call my friend George here, my own private weapon, far more deadly than some. One whiff and strong men give in."

George could be quite cocky, Jack thought to himself. Imagine being a skunk and sharing a desk with the President. Imagine being able to loll back in your chair with your feet on the desk. Just like the President.

Dad nudged Jack and winked. Whispering, he said, "I wonder if George helps the President make decisions. I wonder if he talks on the phone to world leaders."

Mum interrupted them.

"Now, Mr President and Mr George, we would be very grateful if you could arrange for us to get back to England. Jack has school you understand, and we really have been away far longer than we had planned."

"Not so fast, ma'am," said the President.

"Not so fast indeed," said George.

The President continued, "George, my lady wife and myself need your help. We've a little nut for you to crack."

"Or egg to crack," laughed George.

"Steady... steady, George," warned the President. He pressed a button and spoke into a machine. "Ask my lady wife to bring Harriet in, please."

"And who is Harriet?" sighed Mum.

Jack could see she was a bit fed up, just like she got when he came home with his friends and they made a mess. She flopped down on a chair and looked cross. Dad sat beside her and tried to look put out as well – but Jack could tell from the silly grin on his face that he was hiding his own excitement.

The door opened and a very tall woman in a very smart suit walked in.

"George, Harry get your feet off the desk," she snapped.

The President and George jumped to attention. Jack could tell they were both scared stiff, and he didn't blame them. The President's wife was just like his headmistress. Even Mum jumped up.

"Cupcake, please meet our honoured guests – Jack and Jack's mum and Jack's dad," the President said rather feebly.

For some reason, probably because she was so grand looking, Jack's mum curtsied.

"Pleased to meet you, Lady President," she said, putting out her hand politely, but as she did it she suddenly let out a blood-curdling scream.

Jack's dad ran forward. "My darling what is it?" he asked.

Jack's mum couldn't speak, she just pointed at the President's wife.

Sticking out of her blouse – between the buttons – was the head of a parrot. It was an amazing sight.

The tiny bird had a beautiful face and a very large beak. Mum was transfixed – just standing staring at the bosom of the President's wife.

George started to snigger.

"Stop it, George," snapped the President's wife. And he did – at once.

"This is Harriet. Poor little thing, you've scared her half

silly. She's a Red Speckled Parrot from the Amazon."

"That silly Easter Bunny," the President's wife explained, "left us a little egg this April. He told the President it was a special Easter egg for very special people. Well," said the President's wife, "you can imagine our surprise when Harriet hatched out of it on Easter morning. As much as we love animals, the White House is no place for a Red Speckled Parrot. I've been up day and night feeding Harriet from a little doll's bottle, and I'm exhausted. Harriet needs to get back to her home and family. Quite honestly, we've already got a skunk thinking he can run this country. The last thing we need is Harriet joining in."

"But Cupcake," interrupted the President, "we could keep her right here in the Oval Office."

"Absolutely not," replied the President's wife. "We are running a country, not a zoo. Anyway, she's a security risk – I know she's listening to every word we say – before you know it she'll be repeating top secret information to the cleaners. Now, Jack – I can see your mother is a little shocked."

Jack looked at Mum. She was slumped in a chair and she looked pale and crumpled.

"I suggest you all spend the night. The White House laundry can sort out your clothes and we'll drum you up something suitable for the Amazon. Then, first thing tomorrow, our own private plane, Air Force One, will fly you all down to Brazil, with Harriet. All right?"

Mum lifted her head and said quietly, "But Jack has school, he must get home. This really is most confusing."

"If I might say so, Mum," the President's wife said kindly, "your little boy will learn a lot more on this adventure than back in his classroom. How many little boys meet Father and Mother Christmas, see the Smokey Mountains, sit in the Oval Office of the White House, fly on Air Force One and visit the Amazon. School can wait." Then, turning to Jack, she added, "You're on a Mission, Jack."

Jack gasped. Dad stood up.

"Absolutely, Mr and Mrs Cupcake – I mean President. George too, you're dead right. There's a world out there for Jack to see. We'll take Harriet home and we'll do it with pleasure. My wife is tired but a good night's sleep will sort her out."

"You're a brick," said the President's wife. "We'll see that you are treated royally. I will now take you on a guided tour of the White House and tomorrow I'll make sure Air Force One flies over New York so you can see the sights – the Statue of Liberty, the Empire State Building – and then we'll fly you over the Grand Canyon and on to Brazil."

George and the President looked relieved.

"Thank you and good night," they said, as they shook paws and hands with Jack, Mum and Dad.

Chapter Five

Air Force One was a very special plane. It had beds and a dining-room and it had a bathroom with a bath.

Jack, Mum and Dad peered out of the windows as they swung in a large circle over New York. They were bowled over by the Grand Canyon and were stunned at the size of America.

Mum had cheered up a lot and sat happily with Harriet on her lap.

Harriet was very angry with the Easter Bunny. She whispered to Mum in funny little chirps – like someone who was pursing their lips together while trying to kiss. She explained that she was a very rare type of parrot and that the Amazon was such a precious place – in so much danger from humans destroying it that the Easter Bunny should have known better. It was wrong to take eggs from any nest – and the Easter Bunny should stick to chocolate and never try to impress anyone again. A lot of the journey she just snuggled into Mum's chest and gave little snores.

When they arrived in Brazil they were met by a very important-looking man. He said he was the American ambassador. On the journey to the rain forests he told Jack, Mum and Dad that the embassy had contacted the Easter Bunny, who had seemed terribly surprised that the President did not want to keep Harriet, especially as he was so well known as an animal lover. The Easter Bunny had explained which nest and exactly where he had stolen Harriet's egg from and said that he was sorry to have caused such a lot of trouble.

"The Easter Bunny wants big people in big places to think a lot of him – but he made a boo boo this time," said the ambassador, shaking his head.

The drive into the rain forests was exciting. It felt like a never-ending journey through a steamy emerald green wood.

They had been driving for a long, long time when suddenly Jack noticed a tiny white car bumping along behind them. For hours the car followed and Jack started to feel suspicious. He could see a man driving and a woman with curly blonde hair beside him. They looked shifty.

Eventually, Jack turned to the ambassador.

"There is a car behind us that has been following us for ages. I think we're being trailed."

Jack was right.

Every time the black car turned right – the white car turned right and every time the black car turned left the white car turned left.

"Let's have some fun," said the ambassador. "Hold on to your hats, everyone."

The chauffeur put his foot down and the big black car sped forwards, Mum clutched Harriet and Harriet squawked with fright.

They couldn't see out of the windows as there was so much dust billowing up.

"OK, let's turn here," barked the ambassador.

They did.

Suddenly, there was the noise of scrunching, squealing brakes and a huge bang. Jack looked at Mum, expecting her to be terrified. Much to his astonishment, she was not – instead, she had a glint in her eye and a huge grin on her face.

"Let's get them," she shrieked, leaping out of the car before anyone could stop her.

The horrible crunching had been the noise of the white car hitting a huge tree stump. The dust had been so thick that the driver couldn't see where he was going and had driven slap into the trunk.

Jack climbed after Mum and watched as she ran towards the white car. Dad followed. But, just as he shouted, "Careful, Mum, watch out," the woman with the blonde curly hair leapt out of the white car carrying an enormous butterfly net. Mum charged towards her, swinging her handbag like a truncheon, yelling, "You're under arrest." The man jumped out of the driver's seat and started to run away.

"Come on Jack, let's cut him off," Dad whispered. Dad dashed into the fray – Jack couldn't believe the sight – "Wait for me, Dad," he shouted. Trying to escape, the man tripped and as he stumbled Jack lunged forwards and grabbed at his ankles. Dad jumped on top of him.

Meanwhile, Mum and the blonde curly-haired woman were running around and around the tree stump.

Suddenly, from out of the bashed boot of the white car, came an enormous slithering snake. It was huge. It was the hugest snake Jack had ever seen. Jack was sitting on top of the man. Dad was tying the man's wrists with the ambassador's necktie.

Harriet was hiding in the ambassador's top pocket – peeking out.

Mum didn't notice the snake. The snake was so long that its head was nearly at the tree stump while its tail was still somewhere in the boot.

Jack tried to shout, "Mum, watch out!" But he couldn't get his mouth to speak the words. He didn't need to.

The snake knew where it was going. Silently, it slunk towards the woman and then darted forwards, felling her, curling around her legs and pinning her down.

Mum stopped in surprise. Wiping the sweat from her grimy face, she smiled at the snake and said quite calmly, "Thanks so much – a friend in need is a friend indeed."

The woman and the man were questioned by the ambassador. Tied up against the tree trunk they looked very pathetic. Jack listened as they slowly confessed. Yes, they had been following Jack, Mum and Dad. They ran a shady business – which sold very valuable animals to nasty selfish people who liked to show off. The snake was a rare Indian python.

An American film of *The Jungle Book* was being made in the rain forests and the snake, whose real name was Zoë, had been bought from a zoo in New York.

"When I knew I was going to star in *The Jungle Book*," Zoë explained, "I was so excited because I thought I was going home to India. But then I was coiled up and squeezed into a crate and flown to Brazil. Now I'm miserable because I'll never get home – not even back to my friends in New York.

"These vile people here stole me one night and locked me in the boot of their car. I heard them plotting to capture Harriet because they thought she would be priceless. They wanted to sell her to the enemy because they thought she would know all the President's secrets."

Zoë was looking very forlorn.

"It's all turned into a fiasco – my career as a movie star. If I get shoved in one more box, I think I'll go dotty. First, I was put in a box when I was trapped in India and sent to the Bronx Zoo, and then again when I was sent to Brazil to make that silly film. India in the Amazon... my fangs," she sniffed.

Mum wiped Zoë's skin, being careful to go in the same direction as the scales.

"You've got all dusty," she said soothingly. "I'll give you a good polish."

The ambassador cleared his throat.

"You are a national heroine, Zoë," he said. "Who knows what secrets little Harriet could have given away. These horrible froth-spits are nothing but spies – as well as lousy animal jailers. We can get you back to India but we'll need Mum, Dad and Jack as escorts."

"We don't want to go to India," Mum cried out. "We want to get Jack back to school."

Dad looked at Mum. He had a twinkling shine in his eyes that Jack had never seen before.

"I think we should have a little talk," he said, firmly. "Come along, Mum."

Mum and Dad wandered over to a clearing and Jack watched, fascinated. This was not the Mum or Dad that he knew. Dad was speaking with Mum, not being spoken at.

They were having a discussion – this was not something they had ever done before. Once they had finished talking they wandered back arm in arm.

"We will go to India," Dad said.

"Jack doesn't need school as much as Zoë needs to get home," Mum added.

A squeaky voice suddenly broke everyone's thoughts.

"I think you've forgotten about me." It was Harriet.

The ambassador fiddled around in his top pocket and untangled Harriet's claws from his shirt.

According to the Easter Bunny, your nest is just up the road here," he said.

"Bundle those scoundrels into the trunk – let's give them a taste of their own medicine," he told the chauffeur.

"We'll walk Harriet home. Zoë, you get comfortable in the car, stretch out and relax."

Jack, Mum, Dad, the ambassador and Harriet stopped at the bottom of a huge tree. They all kissed Harriet goodbye, she nibbled each of their noses with her beak.

"Now keep out of trouble," the ambassador said in a strict voice. "Remember, careless talk costs lives."

Dad looked at Harriet.

"Go on Harriet, tell us, did you hear any real secrets – top secrets in the Oval Office?"

"Oh yes, oh yes I did," Harriet answered.

All four of them tried to hide their interest.

Then Dad couldn't resist. "Go on – tell us, do," he begged.

"All right," Harriet said, "but not a word to anyone. I don't want to be captured and tortured – but this is what they used to say."

"Who's they?" asked the ambassador.

"Mr and Mrs President, of course," Harriet said. "Mrs President used to say every day –"

"Yes, yes," interrupted Mum. "Go on."

"I'm trying to," said Harriet. "She used to say, 'It's a secret, Cupcake – a wonderful secret, but if those world leaders knew our secret – what keeps this country going is...'"

"What, what is it?" asked the ambassador.

Harriet sighed. "She used to say to the President every day, 'You, my darling Cupcake, are the best kisser in the whole world. It's the kissing that everyone needs and it's the kissing that the others are missing.' That's what their secret was," laughed Harriet and as she laughed she flapped her wings and disappeared into the jungle, calling behind her, "Don't forget, 'It's the kissing that's missing.'"

"A bird in the bush is worth two in the hand," chuckled Mum shaking her head.

Just as they started to amble back, Jack saw a beautiful

toucan up in the branches, way above his head. Its huge beak opened like a giant crab's claw. But instead of squawking which was what Jack was expecting, it started to sing, very beautifully. It made a wonderful echoing bell-like sound and in between each line it would tap its beak on the branch making a hollow drum noise that went on and on and on in Jack's ears.

School can wait
You're needed Jack
There's work to do
There's nuts to crack.

Jack peered at the bird. He had to scrunch up his eyes to see for sure. His mouth fell open in amazement. No one else seemed to have heard the toucan's song. Far away he could tell that the grown-ups were walking on, padding along the furry forest path. And then the toucan spread its wide shiny wings, and flapped into the darkest distance.

Chapter Six

Dad was surprised when Mum agreed to sail to India on a banana boat. Raising her eyes and wrinkling her forehead, she tutted, "Ah well, in for a penny, in for a pound."

Both Mum and Dad felt seasick at the start of the voyage. But they were cured the instant they discovered the sailors' nightly poker game.

Zoë and Jack spent all the time together finding brilliant uses for each other. Zoë would shimmy up the mast with Jack hanging on to her back. Jack would shade Zoë's eyes while she scanned the ocean for land or pirates.

A woman in a sari met them at the dock. Jack could not understand why she was swaying backwards and forwards. He looked around. Everyone was moving.

"Dad," he whispered. "Everything's rolling around, I can't make the ground stay still."

"That's called sea legs, Jack. When you've been on a boat for a long time rolling with the waves you go on doing it when you get off. It's a funny feeling. Sailors have it nearly all the time. But it will stop. It takes a few days. Even when you lie down, you'll still feel as if you're on the sea."

The woman in the sari was very friendly. Her name was Gotami. She explained the plan. She asked Zoë to tell her where she had come from. She had a truck all ready to take her home.

"It's a long journey. Jack, you and your family are welcome to go too, but we felt you would be happier here in Bombay. Zoë will be well taken care of and you can relax and see the sights. Tomorrow we will all go to Agra and look at the Taj Mahal. Then you will return to Bombay and fly straight back to England.

"Mum, can't we go with Zoë?" pleaded Jack.

"Absolutely not," said Mum. "We'll have a rest and a wash, and then see a few nice things. Tomorrow will be nice as the Taj Mahal is one of the seven wonders of the world. And then it's home, Jack – back to school. This is the end of the road."

Jack glanced at Dad. Dad looked sheepish. They both knew Mum had had enough. Zoë looked disappointed, but she was too excited to be really sad.

"Goodbye, my friend, I've really had fun with you. "I'll never forget you." Jack gave Zoë a huge hug. Zoë hugged Jack back, by curling tightly around his body.

They all waved Zoë off – they seemed to wave forever – until the red truck was a speck at the end of a dusty road.

Bombay was a magical city. It smelt of sweet smoke and spicy food. The hotel was very comfortable. Gotami arranged the plane tickets and told them to take a rest.

"I'll be back later to take you on a sightseeing tour," she said.

Mum and Dad went to have a snooze. Jack tried hard to sleep. But he couldn't. He was very sad. His adventure was ending. Tomorrow they would be going home. He shut his eyes squeezy tight and prayed. "Please, please don't let it finish."

Gotami took them to a restaurant for lunch. They had curry. It was like eating meat that burnt your mouth but wasn't hot to touch.

Jack's tongue was exploding. The curry had a very strange taste. With every chew his jaw seemed to hiss – like a tyre letting out air.

"We mustn't be rude, just eat as much as you can," Mum told Jack quietly.

"This afternoon, we will sightsee and then tomorrow fly to Agra to visit the Taj Mahal," said Gotami. "It is very beautiful. A rare and wondrous palace built by a very rich prince out of love for his wife," she explained. "As you are so very fond of animals we will stop to look at the elephants. They are splendid."

After lunch they saw snake charmers in the market place and went for a ride in a rickshaw. Bombay was an exciting place.

That night back at the hotel, a man in a white uniform and a huge turban came to Jack's room and asked how he would like his bath. Jack was confused.

"Not much thanks," he answered.

"No, no," the man said, laughing. "How hot?"

Jack was very surprised. "Well, warmish," he suggested, and to his amazement the man went and ran his bath – and it was warmish.

The next day they were dazzled by the Taj Mahal. It was fantastic. Jack thought it looked like a huge palace made of icing sugar. Outside and down the road were some elephants.

"We are very proud of our elephants," said Gotami. "They do a lot of work. They move large logs and tree trunks, they help us with our building, and we also use them for parades and processions."

Jack looked. Jack stared. He could feel his eyes being pulled towards one elephant like a magnet. He often mucked about with nails and iron filings in Dad's garage, yanking them into a clutch on top of Dad's huge horseshoe-shaped magnet and now he felt as if he was a pile of filings being drawn towards this elephant.

"Why has that elephant got different ears to the others?" Mum questioned. Her voice jerked Jack back to the hot Indian earth.

"Ah, that elephant is called Seva. We were given Seva as a gift from the Kenyan Prime Minister."

"Where is Kenya?" asked Jack.

"Kenya is in East Africa and Seva is an African elephant. The others are Indian elephants."

"She's unhappy. Look, she's crying," Mum blurted out.

Jack, Dad and Gotami looked at Mum in amazement. Mum was never normally rude. Gotami was very proud of these elephants and it was not very polite to tell her whether they were happy or not, Jack knew that.

Gotami, Dad and Jack now stared at Seva. She *did* look unhappy.

"All elephants have teary eyes," explained Gotami.

"But she is crying! Look – look at that tear drop on the earth."

Mum was right. Without thinking, Jack ran forward.

"Oh, Seva, what's the matter?" he asked.

Seva stopped moving tree trunks and slowly turned her head. Her huge eyes filled with even more tears. She shook her enormous face from side to side.

"There's no point, no point," she whispered.

Jack was surprised that this great animal should have such a quiet voice.

"No point in what?" Jack was gentle as for some reason he felt that this large leathery creature needed their help.

"No point in telling you of my misery."

"Oh yes, there is. We are on a Mission. This is an adventure. We have nuts to crack. We've helped hundreds of animals – well, not hundreds, but lots. We've rescued a reindeer, we've saved a skunk, we've done perfectly with a parrot. We've sailed with a snake and we can encourage an elephant to tell us her problems."

"You've done all that?" Seva seemed impressed.

"Yes, we have, and we can help you, too. Please, Seva, please tell me."

"All right. But it's an enormous nut. A huge nut to crack. I don't think you can rescue me, but I'll tell you anyway."

Mum had sidled up beside Jack and said kindly, "A problem shared is a problem aired." She got out her hanky and wiped an enormous tear drop off Seva's trunk.

"Well, I'm an African elephant. That's why I am bigger than the others. I have bigger ears and bigger tusks, too. I come from Kenya. They brought me here in a wooden crate. And when I arrived they covered me in fine cloth and jewels and paraded me around proudly. I was a present from my country to India. But it wasn't fair on me. I had a family, my herd in Africa. I had my friends. We all looked the same. Here I am different. These elephants speak strangely, they don't live in the wild as I did. This herd is kind enough, but it is not my herd. I want to go home."

"Oh, dear, this is not going to be an easy job," muttered Mum.

Jack watched her walk back to Gotami and they started to talk. Suddenly, before Jack could even gasp, Seva wrapped her trunk around his middle. She lifted him high, high in the air and then plopped him on her back. It was the most exciting, stomach-bobbing feeling.

"Look at me, Mum!" Jack shouted.

Mum swung around. "How on earth did you get up there?" she cried. "Oh dear, I knew this would get out of hand."

Gotami put her arm around Mum's shoulder and led her to a shady tree. They plonked down and talked. Jack sat high in his watch tower. He could see for miles. It's much easier to see the world from high up, thought Jack to himself. I'd like to be a bird or a giraffe.

"Can you see Africa?" called Seva.

"No, but we will, we will." Jack was sure of that.

Chapter Seven

Gotami had been on the telephone for a long, long time. She had spoken to the very most important people in India. They all knew about Jack, Mum and Dad. Yes, they had agreed, it was wrong to keep an unhappy elephant, but it was not possible to get her home.

Mum looked worried, Dad was gazing out of the hotel window and Gotami was sitting with her head in her hands. She looked up.

"No aeroplane can make room for Seva. And even if they did it would be almost impossible to get her from the airport to her herd. She refuses to go back into a craft or on to a ship. We are stumped. I'm sorry."

Jack's head was buzzing. He was thinking, thinking so hard he felt his brain might explode.

"If Hannibal crossed the Alps with all those elephants, surely we can get Seva home?" he insisted.

He started to think of *his* home. He was surprised. He kept seeing his playroom. He couldn't think why at this very important time, his brain kept showing him his toy soldiers. In his mind was a picture of his toy army – the soldiers, the tanks, the bomber planes and the jeeps. As if he was watching a film, he went past the shelf, looking at his favourite toys. Then the film slowed down and closed in on the carriers: the huge planes his army used to move jeeps and tanks.

"Do you have an army in India?" asked Jack.

"The finest," said Gotami proudly.

"Do you have carriers – you know big planes that take jeeps and tanks and things?" Jack questioned.

Mum and Dad looked amazed. "You're brilliant," they shouted together, jumping up and hugging him.

"You're brilliant," Gotami echoed. "The boy doesn't need school. He's clever, he's a wizard, he's …"

"Talking of school," Mum interrupted, "if we could get on to the army quickly, perhaps Jack could manage to get home before term ends."

Seva climbed up the ramp that led into the plane very gracefully. Her huge feet were surprisingly nimble. Gotami stood on the tarmac at the airport with the head of the army. It was all coming true – an army carrier flying Jack, Mum, Dad and Seva to Africa.

Seva was lying on a very nice bed of straw which the army had kindly arranged. Jack snuggled down beside her. The straw smelt sweet. It was rustly and tickly.

"It's crackly, Dad, just like the leaves in the wood when we found Blitzen."

"Who's Blitzen?" asked Seva.

"You may well ask," Mum muttered, and then went back to her crossword puzzle.

Jack curled up, cuddling close to Seva's huge African elephant ears and started to tell her of their adventures. But after a bit his eyes began to close and he fell asleep. In his dreams Blitzen, Harry, Harriet, Zoë and Seva were all together and singing in a row. Behind them were Father and Mother Christmas, Harry's ma, pa and Lavinia, the President, George and the President's wife, the American ambassador, the chauffeur and the toucan, Gotami and the head of the army. Just like a huge choir, and conducting them all was Mum – with Dad playing the drums.

School can wait
You're needed, Jack
There's work to do
There's nuts to crack

Dad pounded the drums and the chorus exploded into:

A nut, a nut,
A nut to C-R-A-C-K!

Jack slept and slept. The pilot's voice woke him up.

"Hello Mum, Dad and Jack. Here we are above East Africa. I'm coming down on an airstrip in the Masai Mara, where Seva's herd lives. This is a beautiful, wild part of Africa, full of zebras, lions, hippos and giraffes. Would you like to get out with Seva and have a look around?"

Mum sat bolt upright. "Absolutely not. I will not risk meeting any more animals. I'm staying put and so are the others. Seva can get out here, but not us."

"Oh, Mum," begged Jack. "Can't we just have a little look?"

"From the window only, Jack, and that's final. Once Seva is out safely, Mr Pilot, we'd like to be taken on to Nairobi airport. No messing about. We'll wait at the airport until our plane leaves for London. I'm sorry, but all good things must come to an end."

Dad, Mum and Jack peered out of the windows. It was an incredible sight. The land was browny yellow and burnt by the strong heat of the sun. They flew over hundreds of zebras, who scattered like beetles under a stone when it's lifted. They circled a murky green river, and saw crocodiles sunning themselves on the banks and hippos lounging in the mud. They watched giraffes eating leaves from the tall branches of trees.

As they landed, Mum yelled, "Look at the lions." She was right. A whole pride of lions, lionesses and cubs were lying in the shade of a big tree, tucking into a dead deer. Vultures sat near by, waiting to finish off leftovers.

Seva staggered up and stretched. She nuzzled Mum and Dad with her trunk and said, "I will never be able to thank you enough." The huge door opened, like a giant's mouth, and the ramp came down. Seva turned and ambled down it, stopped, lifted her trunk and trumpeted. She did not look back. Jack watched her trot off out of his life, but not out of his memory – not ever.

Chapter Eight

Jack, Mum and Dad sat on the balcony of the restaurant at Nairobi airport. They were eating sandwiches and drinking Coke. They were not talking. It was as if there was nothing left to say. They were silent, just sitting in the sun and thinking their own thoughts about their incredible adventures.

Some birds were hopping around the tables, picking up the crumbs.

"Cheeky little things," laughed Mum.

"Looking forward to getting home, Mum?" Dad asked, putting his arm around her.

"Yes, yes I am. Home is where the heart is, you know, dear. But it's been nice. I wouldn't have missed it for the world."

"But we had the world, Mum," Jack said quietly. "We saw the whole world."

"And we saw more, far more." Dad's voice was wistful.

Mum's gaze was dreamy, like she had been given something she'd always wanted, but never imagined she'd get. Jack watched her quietly. He'd never known Mum to be so calm. As he looked he noticed her eyes flicker. Then suddenly she went all stiff.

"Are you OK, Mum?" he asked.

"What's that robin doing here?" Mum sat bolt upright.

Dad and Jack looked over and, yes, there was a robin. A little English robin, just like the one Jack and Dad had listened to rustling under the leaves in the woods. Mum sprinkled some of her bread on the table. They sat silently watching. The robin noticed the crumbs and hopped over.

Mum spoke gently. "Would you mind telling us, as we can't help but be a bit curious, what an English robin is doing in Nairobi airport?"

The robin looked up, and cocked his head to one side. They had to lean forwards to hear his little shrill voice.

"I made a terrible mistake. I lived in England, in the beautiful countryside. Last summer I made friends with the swallows. Every day they'd tell me stories of Africa – how warm it was, how exciting. I used to listen enviously, dreading the crisp frosty ground of winter in England. 'Come, come fly with us,' they'd say. 'Come, come with us to Africa.' We would all sit on the telephone wires, high above the barn, and they would tease me. 'You'll never dare, you're a coward. Go on, prove it to us, that you can fly like we can – that you are brave and want to see the world.' Well, I didn't stop to think. A proud cock robin was

I! When summer ended and they all gathered together, they called to me again: 'Come, come fly.' So I did. Oh, it was a terrible, exhausting journey. But I didn't give up. I was battered by the wind and so very tired."

"You poor darling," said Mum. "But foolish too. You should never do something just to prove how brave you are."

"Oh, now I know that," sighed the robin. "I miss England so much. It's too hot here for me. I lost my swallow friends. But I had to stop, I was too tired. I will never make it home. I could never travel that journey again."

Jack was watching Mum very closely. The sides of her mouth were twitching, just a little, but he could see she was starting to smile.

Dad began to get that silly grin on his face.

Mum leant down and picked up her handbag. She tipped it upside down and emptied it out on the table. Tissues, keys, lipstick, pennies, a comb and her purse poured out.

"It's about time I cleared out this mess," she tutted. "Here, Dad, put my purse in your jacket, and my lipstick and keys can go in my coat. Jack, pop my comb in your back pocket. Now I'll just line my bag with tissues."

Jack stared at Mum in fascination as she made a little nest in the bottom of her precious handbag. Then she held it open triumphantly.

"There we are, lots of room. I'll not close it, and you'll have a nice, cosy travelling box."

The robin cocked his head to one side again and hopped on to the edge of Mum's bag. He peered inside.

"Hm, nice job, very nice job," he said. "Perhaps when I get home you could leave the bag in your garden. It would make a perfect nest for us next year."

"We'll see about that," chuckled Mum.

"Oh, what a relief," sang the robin. "Home, sweet home."

He nestled into Mum's bag just in time for them to hear: "Flight 100, Nairobi to London, is now boarding. Please make your way to the gate."

Dad turned to Jack. "Who'd have thought it, Jack? Who'd have ever thought it?" He shook his head and ran his hands through his hair.

"Come along, you two, don't try and stretch this out. The sooner we get home, the sooner we'll all settle down to normal life. And in any case there'll be other adventures I am sure. Standing there shaking your heads isn't going to bring it back and certainly isn't going to make it last any longer." Mum marched towards the plane, trying to look strict, Jack thought, but he knew she was just as sad as they were that the adventure was ending. Her handbag was not quite closed. There was a little crack at the top and Jack noticed she moved it very gently.

As they settled in the seats of the jumbo jet, Mum asked an air hostess if Jack could have a pillow and a blanket.

"He must rest, he has school tomorrow," she explained.

Chapter Nine

The only nuts Jack cracked for the rest of the winter were peanuts for the hungry birds in his garden.

Mum didn't really mind leaving her handbag in the apple tree, although whenever her friends asked what it was doing out there she'd look mysterious and say, "Curiosity killed the cat."

"Talking of cats," said Jack one day, when he heard Mum say this for what seemed like the hundredth time, "can we get a cat? I'd really like a pet, Mum. I feel sort of empty without any animals around."

"No, Jack," she answered flatly. "Cats catch birds. They also sharpen their claws on furniture."

Dad put down his newspaper. "I've just been reading about the Dog's Home. We could get a stray dog, Mum. Look, they've got a photograph here of a mutt they found lost on the road last week."

Mum looked at Dad, a long knowing look.

"Let's see," she sighed, picking up the newspaper. "Oh, poor little mite," she gasped. "It looks so sad."

Dad winked at Jack. "Get your coat, Jack. We're going on a Mission."

Later that afternoon Mum was in the kitchen. The door opened and in shot the most ugly black and white dog she'd ever seen.

"Oh, he's beautiful," she cooed, stretching out her arms, as the dog jumped up. He put his paws on her chest and licked her.

"He's called Flier," Jack said. "Isn't he a corker? We're going up to the woods" – Jack's words were tumbling out with excitement – "to take him for a walk."

"Oh no, you're not", said Mum. "Oh no, not without me. Remember what happened the last time you two went for a walk in those woods. I think I'd better get my coat and come too."